Toads on Toast

Linda Bailey • Colin Jack

Kids Can Press

Fox was bored. Every day it was the same.
Walk to the pond. Catch a big fat toad.
Bring it home. Skin it. Boil it. Eat it.
"I need a change," said Fox.

He headed for the cookbook store.
The toad section was amazing! Who
knew there were so many ways to
cook a toad?

As Fox turned the pages,
he noticed something surprising.
Every single recipe called for
small toads, young and tender.

"Gee," said Fox. "So that's
where I've been going wrong."

That evening, he set out for the
pond as usual. But this time, instead of
looking for a big fat toad, he looked for
small toads, young and tender.

It was hard work.
Those toadlets were *fast*!

By the time Fox got home, he was all puffed out. But he was carrying a lovely bouncing sack of fresh young toads for dinner.

"This is going to be soooo great!" said Fox as he dumped the toads into a bowl. He opened the first cookbook.

Suddenly a huge mother toad came rocketing through the window.

"Stop!" she cried. "What are you doing?"

"I'm *trying* to concentrate," said Fox. "Now let's see. Toad Muffins, Toad Soup, Toad Stir-Fry ..."

SPLAT!

Mamma stared, aghast, at her babies.
"You're going to *eat* them?"
"Ah," said Fox, "here's a good one. Toad Legs."

"Nooooooo!" said Mamma. "Not their legs!
They have such *beautiful* legs."
"I noticed," said Fox, licking his lips.
"Especially the weensy ones."

"Stop!" cried Mamma, throwing herself across the book. "Take ME instead."

Fox thought about it. But the recipes were clear. "You're too old and stringy," he said. "Sorry." And he reached for his knife.

"Ack!" cried Mamma Toad. "Wait! There must be a better recipe. Their poor little legs are so thin. Hardly a mouthful."

Fox glanced at the toadlets and frowned. It was true that their legs were quite scrawny.

Mamma glanced at the toadlets, too. She was *not* pleased.
"Calvin!" she bellowed. "Get away from that butter!"
"Why?" said Calvin.
"Because I said so," said Mamma.

"Hey," said Fox, "here's a good recipe. Toads on Toast. Looks easy, too."

Mamma hopped over to take a peek.

"Well, maybe," she said. "Do you have garlic?"

"Yes," said Fox.

"Bread?"

"Yes."

"Pepper?"

"Yes."

"Truffle oil?"

"Truffle oil!" Fox peered at the book. "It doesn't say anything about truffle oil."

"Well, it *should*," said Mamma. "Everyone knows you can't make Toads on Toast without truffle oil. Where'd you get that crummy book anyway?"

"Uptown," said Fox, with a frown.

"Listen," said Mamma. "I'm going to help you out. I have a *better* toad recipe — a secret, favorite recipe that's been passed down in my family. You're going to love it."

"What's it called?" asked Fox.
"Toad-in-a-Hole," said Mamma.
"Hmmm," said Fox.
"It has toast," said Mamma. "You *like* toast, right?"

"Oh, yes," said Fox, rubbing his paws together. "I do love toast."

"Well, *you* slice some bread," said Mamma, "while I see to my kids. Brucie! Loretta! Get OUT of that honey pot!"

"Ready!" said Fox.
Mamma hopped over.
"Excellent," she said. "This
bread is *perfect*. Just make a
hole in the center."
"Goody," said Fox. "This
is easy."
"Next," said Mamma, "you
butter the bread and put it in
a frying pan. Erleen and Elvis!
Stand back!"
"Yum," said Fox. "I love
butter."

"And now," said Mamma, "you break an egg and pour it into the hole."

"An egg?" said Fox. "Not a toad?"
"An egg," said Mamma firmly. "Then add salt and pepper —"

"No toads?" asked Fox again.

"Trust me," said Mamma. "Now flip it over and sprinkle some parmesan cheese."

"Heeeeey ..." said Fox. "Wait a minute! There's something funny going on here. What about ... the TOADS?"

"Try it without," said Mamma.

Fox grumbled a little. He pouted and stared at the toadlets. But he did take a nibble. Then a bite. And then —

"Wow!" said Fox. "This is delicious!"

"You see?" said Mamma. "It doesn't really *need* toads. That's the secret."

"By golly, you're right," said Fox. "I'm going to make another one."

And so he made another, and another, and another — enough for everyone. Mamma Toad set the table, and they all sat down to eat.

And Fox, being a lazy fox, never again went to the trouble of looking through his recipe books. He didn't bother to catch any more toads, either.

And later, when he had children of his own,
he passed Mamma's secret recipe on to them.
Toad-in-a-Hole became a favorite recipe in the
Fox family ...

... and it can be a favorite in *your* family, too.
(As long as you don't add toads!)

For Lia and Tess, in memory of all those toad-in-a-hole breakfasts — L.B.
For my two little toads, Gabriel and Eli — C.J.

Text © 2012 Linda Bailey
Illustrations © 2012 Colin Jack

Kids Can Press acknowledges the financial support of the Government of Ontario, through the Ontario Media Development Corporation's Ontario Book Initiative; the Ontario Arts Council; the Canada Council for the Arts; and the Government of Canada, through the CBF, for our publishing activity.

Published in Canada by
Kids Can Press Ltd.
25 Dockside Drive
Toronto, ON M5A 0B5

Published in the U.S. by
Kids Can Press Ltd.
2250 Military Road
Tonawanda, NY 14150

www.kidscanpress.com

The artwork in this book was rendered digitally.
The text is set in FG Nando Bold.

Edited by Tara Walker and Yvette Ghione
Designed by Marie Bartholomew

This book is smyth sewn casebound.
Manufactured in China, in 12/2012, through Asia Pacific Offset, 3/F, New factory (No.12), Jing Yi Industrial Center, Tian Bei Estate, Fu Ming Community, Guan Lan, Bao An, Shenzhen, China

CM 12 0 9 8 7 6 5 4 3 2

Library and Archives Canada Cataloguing in Publication

Bailey, Linda, 1948-
Toads on toast / written by Linda Bailey ; illustrated by Colin Jack.
ISBN 978-1-55453-662-7
I. Jack, Colin II. Title.

PS8553.A3644T63 2012   jC813'.54   C2011-908168-7

Kids Can Press is a Corus™ Entertainment company